This Book

Belongs To

FOR MUM

C M Gifford Publishing

All Rights Reserved
Copyright(c) 2022 Chris Gifford

ISBN 978-1-7398854-1-0
Author and Illustrator
Chris Gifford

Artistic Director - Sue Gifford

 chrisgiffordauthor/illustrator

 chrisgiffordauthorillustrator

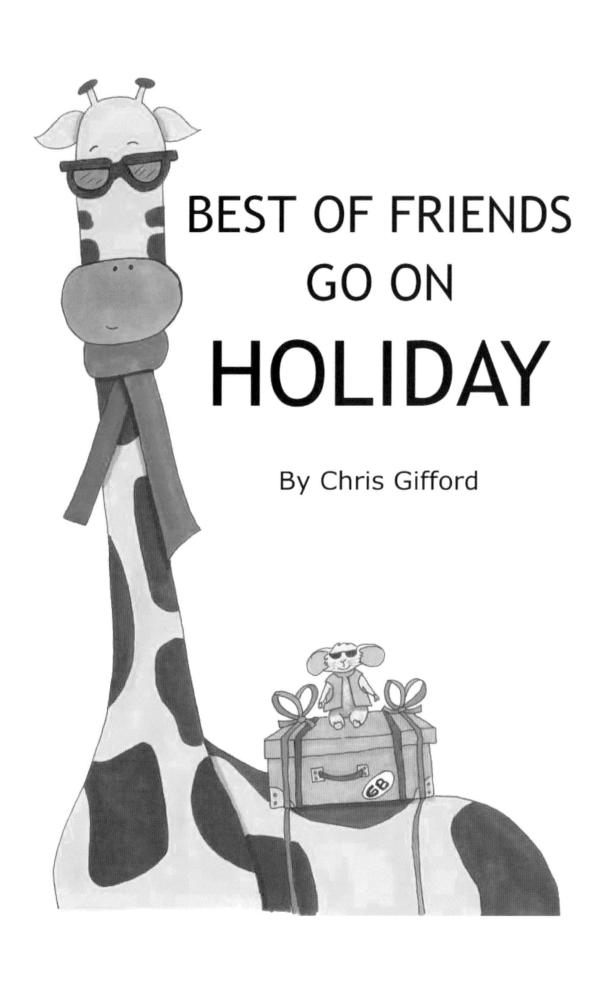

BEST OF FRIENDS GO ON HOLIDAY

By Chris Gifford

Holidays are great and lots of fun.

For Mouse and Giraffe, it's their very
first one.

Giraffe gets the suitcase,

but what should they pack?

An umbrella?

Some

flipflops?

Maybe a rain mac?

Mouse has a think and scratches his head.

"Giraffe, can we take our big comfy bed?"

Giraffe looks at the suitcase
and wonders for a bit.

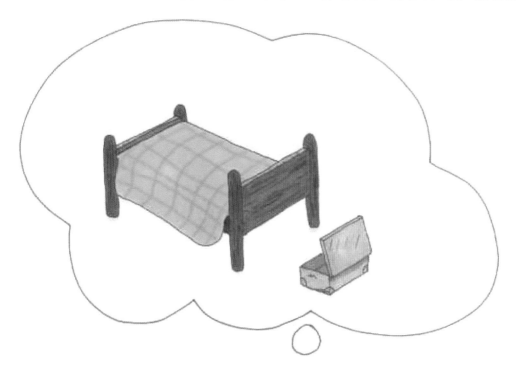

"Mouse"
he says,
"I just don't
think it will
fit!"

Finally, a decision has been made.

They
pack...

 sunglasses,

some sandwiches

and a
bucket
and
spade

They travel to the beach in
their electric car.

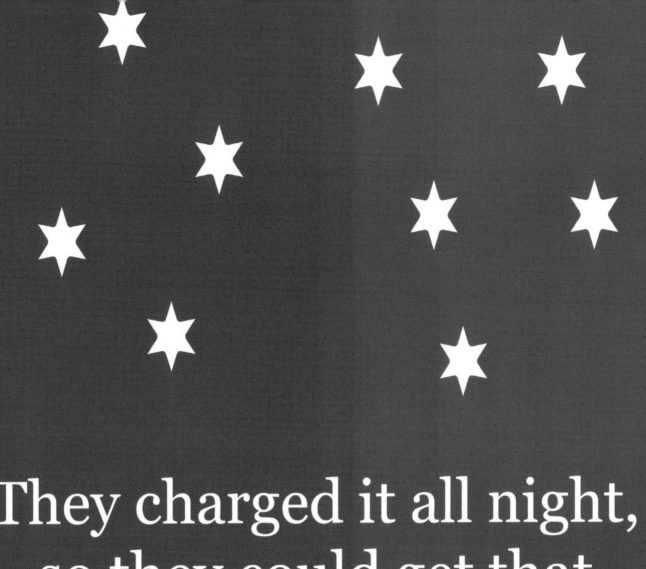

They charged it all night,
so they could get that
far.

They pass a fun fair with a huge ride

and see Snake and Ape on a big slide.

Finally, in the distance they see a beautiful blue. "It's the sea!" Cries mouse.

They sit on the beach and enjoy the sea breeze.
Giraffe eats a leaf sandwich and Mouse has cheese.

Mouse asks,

"Shall we build something with our bucket and spade?"

Giraffe replies,
"Yes!"

But can you
guess what they
made...

That's right!

A sandcastle tall and
proud.

But up in the sky is a big dark cloud.

Raindrops begin to fall, and the sandcastle gets flatter...

and flatter!

"Do not worry Mouse, these things do not matter."

"A holiday is fun in any kind of weather and a holiday is always great, when we are together."

COMING NEXT

BEST OF FRIENDS GO TO HOSPITAL

By Chris Gifford

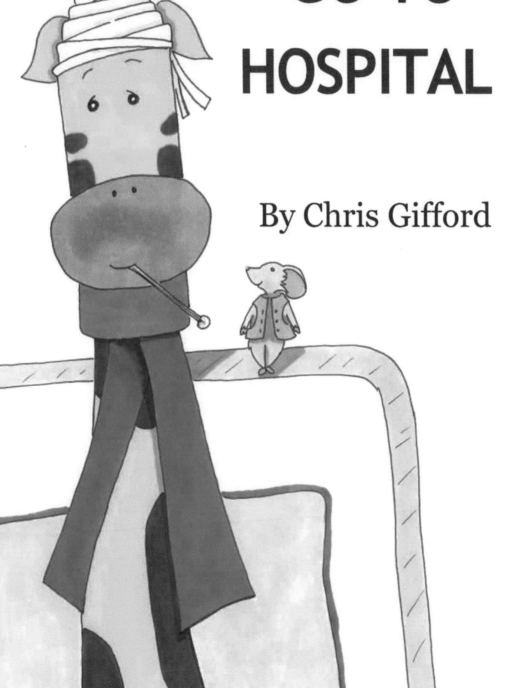

Printed in Great Britain
by Amazon